A Birthday Present for Mom

By Alan Trussell-Cullen
Illustrated by Jane Wallace-Mitchell

 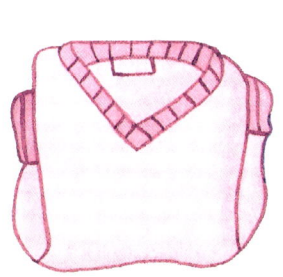 

Chapter 1	Sam's Bedroom	2
Chapter 2	What Will Sam Buy?	8
Chapter 3	Happy Birthday, Mom!	12

Chapter 1

Sam's Bedroom

Sam's mom was starting a new job.
She told Sam he would have to
keep his room clean now.

"I won't have time to pick up your things,
or put your clothes away,
or clean your closet,
or make your bed.
You'll have to do it all by yourself now,"
she said.

Sam tried to clean his room
by pushing everything into his closet,
but the door wouldn't shut properly.
If he opened the door, everything fell out.

Sam tried to put his clean clothes away.
He stuffed the clothes into his drawers,
but then the drawers wouldn't close.

Sam's bed was always covered with books and toys.
Sam *did* make his bed,
but he made it *Sam's way*.
He just pulled the quilt over everything!

Sam knew he should clean his room properly.
Whenever he walked across his floor,
he stepped on things.
Sometimes they hurt his feet!
When he sat on his bed, he sat on things.
When he opened his closet,
things fell out on top of him.

Sam didn't have time to clean his room today.
Tomorrow was Mom's birthday,
and he hadn't made a present for her yet.

"I know," he said.
"I'll buy her something."

What Will Sam Buy?

Sam went down to the shops
on the first floor of the apartment building.
He saw a picture frame.

"Mom could put a picture of our family
in that frame and put it on her desk
at her new job," he said to himself.

He asked the woman how much it cost.

"Twenty dollars," said the woman.

Sam only had four dollars and fifty cents.

"Bye-bye, picture frame," said Sam.

Sam went into the next shop.
He saw some beautiful flowers.

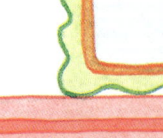

"Mom could put those flowers on her desk at her new job," Sam said to himself.

He asked the woman how much they cost.

"Ten dollars," said the woman.

"Bye-bye, flowers," said Sam.

Sam went home and sat on his bed.

"What am I going to do about
Mom's birthday present?" he said to himself.

Then he had a wonderful idea.
He made a sign that said:

Then he closed the door.

When Mom came home from work,
she heard strange noises coming from Sam's room.
She read the sign on his door and began to wonder
what was going on.

Chapter 3
Happy Birthday, Mom!

The next morning, Sam rushed into the kitchen.

"Happy birthday, Mom!
Come and see your present!"

Sam led Mom to his bedroom and showed her the new sign on the door.

Happy Birthday, Mom!
This is to help you
in your new job.

When Mom opened the door and looked inside, she couldn't believe her eyes.

"Wow!" she said.
"You've cleaned your room!"

She opened Sam's drawers and looked inside.

"You've folded all your clothes, too, and put them away neatly."

She opened Sam's closet door.
This time nothing fell out.

"You've cleaned your closet, too," said Mom.

Then she saw Sam's bed.

"Oh, no!" she said.
"Don't tell me you've made your bed *Sam's way?*"

Sam just laughed.
Mom lifted the quilt and looked underneath.

"You *have* made your bed,
but you've put all your things away
and have made it properly!"

"This is wonderful," said Mom.
"It's the best birthday present I've ever had!"

She gave Sam a great big hug.